IN THE SHADOW OF TRUTH AND OTHER STORIES

Jeremy Lowley

FELIX

Felix Publishing 2020

Email: info.felixpublishing@gmail.com

Print copies available from publisher or online book stores.

In the Shadow of Truth and Other Short Stories

Author Jeremy Lowley 2020 lowley.jeremy@gmail.com

ISBN: 978-1-925662-62-7   Print

ISBN: 978-1-925662-63-4   Digital

Other books by the author:

This Too Shall Pass

Plays:

49 Not Out

The Lady in Suite 57

Two for the Price of One

Registration: Thorpe-Bowker, Level 1 607 St Kilda Rd, Melbourne, Victoria 3000 Australia bowkerlink@thorpe.com.au

IN THE SHADOW OF TRUTH AND OTHER STORIES

Jeremy Lowley

Dedication:

To my father Jack Lowley one of the greatest actors ever known.

TABLE of CONTENTS

IN THE SHADOW OF TRUTH.

JEREMY LOWLEY

Samantha Llewellen got off the Leckhampton Hill, number 14, double decker bus, as she had, virtually every day since she had inhabited this fragile planet. She gazed down the road at the local Catholic Church, St Philipps and St James, known by all and sundry as "Pip and Jim's cannon fodder".

Samantha had attended the church since she was a wee child and had confessed her life's misdemeanors by pouring her innocent heart out to a number of priests about her rather, predictably unblemished life. Oh, but the memory of that tartan scarf that had somehow found its way into her hand bag. Ah, the guilt, the overpowering shame.

She never, ever, wore the tainted thing! But she said a lot of Hail Marys without even being told to. She had arrived at the glorious age of eighteen years, and was open minded and intelligent enough to make her own mind up about most things, but every now and then she was quite happy to ask for a little guidance. This was one of those instances.

It was tricky!!

Unhappily, her dear Uncle Harry had passed away recently, and Sammy had been asked to act as executor of his will.   She had immediately agreed to the position, and told the family solicitor, that she would be honored.

Apart from anything else, she was a very precise girl and would go through her Uncle's things meticulously, especially his diaries. She already knew that her Uncle had led a somewhat colorful past, but that didn't bother Sammy in any way, she simply adored him, and graciously forgave him for any misgivings that he might have committed during his hectically rarified life. After all, hadn't he been the first one to allow her to enjoy a glass of champagne when she was just twelve years old, having whispered to her not to tell anyone, especially his rather austere wife, the righteous Auntie Edith.

Sammy rather assumed that he may have had a secret past life that made him a little bit more exciting than the, run of the mill, family that she was part of. She decided to start at the very beginning.

So, here goes.

During the difficult post war period, England, like most other countries, went through a very challenging time. Nearly all young men in Britain were expected to commit to national service for their country; whether they liked it or not. And inevitably of course, Uncle Harry was no exception. So it was, that boys aged between eighteen and twenty-three years, were expected to serve their queen and country.

During that befuddled time, Most of the English regarded National service as a throwback to the commitment demanded of them after the end of the dubious two world wars. Nevertheless, a lot of guys would, if given half a chance, accept their time in the forces as part of the maturity process. In many instances they got to travel abroad to the various British outposts; in fact some rather exotic spots that they had only heard about in history/geography lessons. So, this was probably the first time they had been away from home, and their mummies' guiding influences.

Oh, the trouble some of them got into!!!

At this stage in the creative history of Great Britain, it was accepted that the female of the species was not expected to join those heroic few lads.   Undoubtedly the girls were becoming emancipated, but had not reached those dizzying heights yet, and, rather sensibly, probably never would accept National Service as a means of attaining maturity. During his stint in the 'Nachos', it was discovered that Uncle Harry had an ability with electronics that made him especially valuable. Not only was he an excellent radio operator, he was capable of servicing and repairing the transmitter, even in the field.

In his youth, he had actually made a crystal wireless set whilst still at school and presented it to the family, so he had absolutely no fear of the new industry, ambitiously named computerized electronics. So it was that Sammy settled down to the task of absorbing Uncle Harry's meticulously recorded diaries from front to back.

Boy oh boy, there was some juicy stuff in it. She wondered if Auntie Edith had read them. Don't really think so.

Oh dear, this was a biggie!!

No wonder Uncle kept them in a secret place. Samantha, somewhat smilingly, imagined that there would be quite a number of little Egyptians running around who spoke English with a pronounced North Yorkshire accent.

As Samantha read through the precisely worded diaries, she quickly realized just what a disciplined man her Uncle really was. For some unexplained reason, he was exceptionally diligent about his time in the Army Communications Corps. The diaries contained information that only another radio operator could find even remotely interesting.

For instance, radio wave lengths, volume control dials, battery strengths, Morse code jargon, etc., etc. Rather boring stuff, unless, of course, it was lifesaving information, in which case it would immediately become more than a wee bit important.

Sammy ploughed on with the literal assurance that something would come to mind which would colour Uncle Harry's story beyond the rather mundane detail that was in the first chapters of his tale.   Things like, how heavy the radio was how close he had to get to the dangerous front, what protection he was allowed- apparently, not a lot!!!

In many ways the necessary isolation he felt from his fellow infantrymen, plus the extra danger he faced, forced him to accept that he had to be at least as fit as the front-line soldiers, and for much the same reason, self-preservation!

His job was simply to relay information back to the command post which could be up to two miles behind the lines.   They would in turn, direct whatever support was required on the front. So, he helped to provide a vital form of data that made modern warfare possible, and much safer, at least, for one side!

In retrospect, none of it really made any sense at all to Harry. Samantha got the distinct impression that in some ways Uncle Harry rather enjoyed some of the exciting elements of combat duty. His writings mentioned a lot of the places in which they operated. And yes, during this period, it was always somewhere in the Middle East.

However, the British were not always welcomed with open arms. For many reasons, some of the countries had turned against the Brits', Uncle Harry seemed to believe that it was just one more facet of war that could never be successfully explained. So, don't try.

This period turned out to be a crucial time in the chronicles of English history. UK was desperately trying to tidy up the remnants of WW2, but also trying to reconnect with people who had been once been reliable friends. During his rather fanciful times, Harry occasionally mused that challenging ones foes to a game of soccer would have been much more creative avenue to peace.... even if they had to lose a few games of football... so what, over the years the English had become rather good at losing the odd match or two, or three.

Just a pipe dream really!

What, lose at soccer?   Well not to the bloody French!   Really, no one's that forgiving!

Sammy very quickly realized from his notes, that the inevitable tedium that had to be faced was almost as bad as the scary danger that needed to be, danced with, if found at the front. And then, without any warning to find oneself in the middle of completely unexpected   danger. Hot, dry, dusty, and utterly terrified.

Not a good time to get complacent!!

Samantha began to realize that Uncle Harry's scribblings became part of the man that she admired so much. Like all diary writers he obviously didn't expect anyone else to read them. They were private thoughts, and his alone!! He also went on to admit, rather sadly, that his soccer aspirations wouldn't really work.

A shame!

Well, maybe one day!

His second year in the forces took him to a much darker and more worrying part of the world, indeed, map wise, closer to the land of his birth.

Welcome to Northern Ireland!

Geographically very close to England in every way, yet still without the resolve that the two countries so desperately needed to find a peaceful outcome to what was a historic tsunami. Peace now, was as much an obvious pipe dream as it had been for well over four hundred years. Very little had changed, maybe the guns were more automatic and much deadlier, but the hatred and horrifying mistrust was probably more profound now than it had ever been.

The times were euphemistically called 'the troubles'. An understatement if ever there was one. Uncle Harry arrived in Ulster on the twelfth of May. Samantha tried to understand how things had changed.

She read on - Harry painstakingly recorded that Ireland was as cold and bleak as Saudi Arabia had been hot and dry. He joyfully wrote that he would only be in Ireland for three months before he was due for discharge from the forces - NOT LONG NOW- he scribbled in capital letters.   He'd had enough!!

It was equally obvious that Uncle harry thought that the Middle East was much more dangerous than Ireland would ever be. It took approximately ten days in Belfast before he learned the startling truth.

With a shaking hand Samantha read the next diary input.

It was the twenty first of May, a dismal rainy day, but not unlike most of the others that made up Northern Ireland in early spring. His army uniform helped to keep the cold out. Harry looked around at the semi-detached dwellings and smilingly recognized that the narrow roads and small houses reminded him of his home town Leeds, in Yorkshire, North Riding, of course.

He quickly ran to the corner store and bought a packet of Senior Service 'ciggies'. They would be enough for now. He sauntered down the tightly packed street and went past house number sixty-one.

He thought he heard a noise that was now familiar to him. It was the breaking of a window and the whooshing sound of something being thrown at him. He immediately saw the gray/ metallic/ blue of a hand grenade land within two feet of his army boots.

His basic training and natural speed coupled with a strong element of self-preservation enabled him to dive on the bloody thing and, in one movement, randomly throw it as far as possible. He had no real idea where the damn thing landed, all he knew was that it exploded somewhere in his vicinity- the noise was deafening... He lay there shuddering and stunned, in an alien, but oddly, silent world. Within three minutes, his platoon had caught up with him and dragged him behind a brick wall for protection.

Sergeant Mallory quickly checked him over. Physically He appeared to be alright, the Sergeant, rather gently, asked him some questions. His full name. His squadron. Where, and if, he remembered his home town. Questions that in normal circumstances were blatantly obvious. But not if you were in deep rattled shock. Harry just stared at Mallory. Once they realized that he was basically in one piece. They loaded him into an armored car and drove him back to headquarters.

Samantha was pleased to read on, that her uncle had, oh so narrowly, missed becoming one more statistic of war. No one in the family knew just how close he came to, a 'telegram from the war office.'

The more Sammy read, the more obvious it became to her, that Uncle Harry hadn't the faintest idea what happened; but he instinctively believed that something horrifying had occurred at number sixty-one. Sammy ploughed on and read that two weeks passed before her uncle was in a fit state to understand the dire ramifications of May the twenty first!

Whilst he was still in hospital Colonel McGregor came to visit him. It turned out that McGregor was a well-educated, and trained, medical/military man who methodically probed Uncle Harry with searching questions. Simple, rather obvious ones.

Uncle Harry wrote that he had no idea why they interrogated him, apart from anything else, they already knew the answers to most of their questions - so what the hell!!

It made little sense to Harry's rather precise mind, in fact it made no bloody sense at all, but McGregor was the boss and Harry had learnt that the British army usually had fairly good reasons for doing things - so!

They were in the middle of a cup of tea when the colonel suddenly asked him what he really thought happened on that twenty first day of May.

Harry shook his head, and with genuine honesty, said, "I really have no idea sir; I was hoping you might be able to tell me".

McGregor stared at him for quite a while before he answered. "Well, this is what I know from the reports I've read, a thrown grenade ended up in the house next door to number sixty one. You must, have worked out by now, that the grenade triggered of at least two other small bombs and the house was pretty much demolished."

Samantha read the next short diarized sentence with mounting horror.

Harry rather dramatically demanded. "What exactly happened sir, I've got to know." McGregor answered as he thoughtfully stirred two lumps of sugar into his cuppa. "Well it's what we call a spot house. We believe that at least four grenades were stored there, almost certainly by the IRA - and indeed would be an obvious and rather deadly trap. It's almost certain that a grenade triggered the others off, and of course, inevitably blew the house to pieces. We are in no way sure about how the grenade ended up in the house."

McGregor continued to stare at Harry for a long time, trying to read his mind, but before he could ask the question that was teetering between the two of them - McGregor very solemnly said. "The house was pretty much razed to the ground - two people perished in the explosion." McGregor whispered. "A mother and her young daughter, we don't really have any other information. But I trust you understand that, as a consequence, we need to get you out of Ireland as quickly and quietly as possible... There will be people who are searching for you. You will be leaving here in three days' time----we have already booked you on a flight back to England. Don't ask to where, at this stage we are not prepared to tell you, and of course you will not be able to contact any of your family, at least for a while."

"I presume that this must seem very - secret service to you. Well it's not, it's entirely for your benefit. I will catch up with you before you leave". McGregor cleared his throat by coughing. "I have some idea how disturbing this must be to you. There is no alternative." McGregor smiled at Harry. "You must know that we will try to support you for - well as long as it takes. Ok, that's it - good morning to you."

Samantha at last began to realize that Harry must have come back to England and never once mentioned his experiences in Northern Ireland to anyone. Not even his immediate family. And indeed, he must have felt somewhat isolated and apprehensive to confide in anyone close to him.

He didn't know who to trust.

Sammy was very disturbed by the knowledge of Uncle Harry's army hostilities. She knew him to be a pacifist who disapproved of violence in just about every way. He occasionally spoke of the destruction caused by randomly dropping bombs on people that you can't even see from an aeroplane. He also came to believe that bullets were very simply small 'bombs' - nothing more, nothing less!! Hence, she found it difficult to connect the uncle she loved and admired so much with the story in his diaries.

The worst part was not being able to talk to anyone who might understand exactly what had happened in Ireland all those years ago, but she felt compelled to honour her Uncle's story by keeping it to herself------

A lonely place at times!!

Three months later, the will had been read and details pretty much cleared up. Sammy still felt, betwixt and between. The diaries had caused her to question a lot of the values that she held so dear in her young life. How to clear her conscience---what to do? ---who to tell? ---if anyone!! It took a while before she decided that she must face her doubts and unburden her conscience.

Sammy decided that she would talk with her local priest… in effect, make a confession. Something she had not done for many years.

She had known Father Dion for a while and felt reasonably at ease with him. He was a youngish man, who had blended into the village life very well, he enjoyed the reputation of having a relatively modern outlook on things ecclesiastic. Anyway, he played bass guitar in a local jazz band, and apparently enjoyed a beer or two. So… maybe a person you could talk to!

Sammy sat in the tiny nave of, St Pip and St Jim's church waiting her turn to unburden her disturbed thoughts. Father Dion smiled at Sammy and beckoned her to follow him into the confessional box. After the preliminaries were finished, they started to talk, almost like old friends. Sammy eventually blurted out her story about Uncle Harry's diaries and just how horrifying she found the truth of his actions. Father Dion smiled gently at Sammy and told her that he understood her need to unburden her soul.

"You must, I believe, try not to feel guilty about the unique knowledge that you have been given. Equally, I hope that you understand that I'm unable to discuss anything with you of my conversations with your Uncle Harry. His confession is sacred to me and always privileged. But I can tell you that we met quite often, and he had told me of his experiences". A very long pause before Dion sighed and explained. "I must tell you that, with all my training, I feel the same sense of shock at discovering the disturbing past of some of my flock as anyone else. However, I was able to convince your Uncle that his story was safe with me. It would never go further; but I appreciate your shock at discovering the past of someone you loved. The truth is often very difficult to accept, indeed, it's because one feels such strong emotions that belief is sometimes stretched by unattractive facts.

Your uncle told me about Northern Ireland and the horrors he faced there. I believe that he trusted me and so, gave me the very short memorandum that he kept from all those years ago. I still have it by the way."

Sammy stared at Father Dion and told him that she had read all three diaries, and the other letters that were with them. The Father shook his head and said. "No, no you can't have read this one I've had it in my possession, for over two years now."

Samantha looked questioningly at the priest for quite a long time.   She shook her head before admitting to him that her feelings were entirely rattled by what Father Dion had just told her, she was simply confused, and very lost.

Father Dion, at last spoke to Sammy and told her that he believed that Harry would have wanted her to read his last diary, the Father very seriously said. "Actually, it's not really a diary but a report from an army official. I think it may help you come to terms with this very bewildering situation.   That's all I can tell you." He smiled as he reminded Sammy. "Of course, you know, I'm always here, every day, wet or dry, good or bad, especially on Sundays - whether we beat Manchester United or not, ha ha . He smiled as he said goodbye to her, and tentatively pushed the rather battered envelope towards Samantha.

She drove home and very sensibly poured a large glass of Chardonnay, sipped an equally large glug of the wine, and settled down to read the contents. After fifteen minutes, a wry smile came over Sammy's face. "So that's what happened. Now I think I understand!!!"

It was nearly two months later when she saw Father Dion again, it was in the local supermarket, and they pretty much locked eyes at the same time.   Sammy smiled a slightly cheeky grin and waved to Father Dion. She shouted over to him. "How's your team going?" Father pretended to cry then burst into laughter. "You've got to have a lot of faith in my job, especially in the football season. Everything alright with you?"

Sammy sighed "Oh yes, yes, I feel much more settled now anyway, I support Leeds United. So!! Goodbye Father - and, by the way, thank you.

I'll always be grateful to you."

HOW T0 SHOOT YOUR BEST FRIEND.

JEREMY LOWLEY

JONATHON.

Jonathon walked into the dark forest; his shoes were filthy... Well or course they were, it had been raining for at least two hours. He idly kicked at the broken branches lying around the forest floor, which made his shoes even muckier. He stumbled across a rock that was approximately a similar size and shape to that of his arse, so he sat on the damned thing, an extra-large sigh escaped through his tired lips and mingled with the damp air.

What a bloody mess he had made of his life so far!

The sodding bank had foreclosed his mortgage and taken over the house. When only six months earlier, they had almost forcibly offered him an extra mortgage because "He was such a good risk."

Yeah right!

 Veronica, his wife of nearly fourteen years, had finally decided that she was, and had always been, a practicing lesbian.   It was only after all those years of diligent practice that she discovered that she was really quite good at it! Obviously, all that bloody hockey whilst at St Albans school...Yes that was it.

It couldn't be his fault...

No way.   No of course not.

Worst thing was she had buggered off with their next door neighbour.   Actually he quietly thought Faye was a right little raver...I guess she couldn't make up her mind if she was the 'sun or the moon, or the son of the moon'. But Veronica hadn't even had the decency to take their ill-mannered kids with her...selfish bitch!

Leonard Compton, his general manager, had explained, very carefully, exactly why they had to let him go....It wasn't anything to do with him personally; and definitely not the fact that his department had made a loss of two point eight million dollars the previous year! Oh dear me no.

Good old Leonard had stressed that, at least twice, but then wished him all the very, very best of luck in the future. As they shook hands for the very, very last time. He shouted after him, "Don't forget that you have a wonderful talent with a camera in your hand, no, I really mean it. You've got genuine skills. Just learn how to look at life through a 50mm lens; you'll get it, one day".

How in the hell did old man Compton know about his love of photography?

Jonathon considered his life and pondered, not for the first time. "Poverty is no cure for a democracy of one.''   But it was a compellingly damned good argument!

The Boyo checked his pockets and realised that he only had nineteen dollars and twenty-five cents with him. His car needed petrol and that wouldn't even get him back home. At least he still had his camera with him.

What to do? He looked at his filthy shoes and a wry smile came over face...

Yes of course that's the answer!

IF YOU DONT PLANT SEEDS, FLOWERS CAN'T GROW.

My god I can't believe it's this cold! Only three weeks earlier Melinda had been sunbathing on the Sunshine beach near Noosa Heads. Melinda had always found the anonymity of the beach really relaxing, Apart from anything else she believed that the gentle exercise of swimming every day and the warmth of the early morning sunshine had the most efficacious effect on her.

Many years earlier.

"Onwards and upwards" That's what Mr Granzzia had said, and he should know. Well he should shouldn't he! And that's what Melinda had thought, well of course she did! But that was a long time ago, Things change. At the time, it all made sense to Melinda who had always trusted in the "powers that be" since she was an innocent twelve year old. It was also, incidentally, how she broke her leg in two places and discovered that she could not trust Mr 'onwards and upwards' Granzzia. Or ever water-ski again. Bloody nuisance, as that was pretty much all she was really good at.

It was whilst she was recuperating on the beach that she met Mike Hargreaves. Surely the most beautiful man that had ever walked the face of the earth. And that wasn't just her opinion; well obviously, it was his as well! But Mike had more or less got her to believe in herself. Told her; in no uncertain terms that water skiing was over. But that she was ideally trained and psychologically ready to take on another sport.

Downhill snow gymnastics - downhill bloody gymnastics! Oh, come on mate, you've got to be bonkers! This is Queensland in the middle of summer!

It was almost eighteen months after their first meeting that she realised her own natural talents and the training programme that Mike- ''I don't care about him anymore. Robert Redford was far more smashing anyway'' promoted. That her basic skills and inner strengths came to the fore.

 She was a natural. Within six months she was doing all the downhill moves that were expected of her, but much more than that, she had developed moves and double twists and even somersaults that were all her own.... She didn't know it. But she was on her way.

Oddly enough it turned out that, whilst Brisbane was singularly lacking in snow, even in winter. The QLD Institute of Sports had the best gymnastics curriculum in Australia, if not in the world.

Over the next eight years she had strengthened her body and developed confidence [which she secretly believed came from her lack of fear, born of water skiing], until the fateful day that she was actually invited to join the Aussie team and compete at the World Winter Games and then maybe the Olympics.

Travel the world and compete against the best... "Yup, that'll do me."

Melinda had never actually won a gold medal. But she always came second or third.... Anyway, hells bells, she always made the top ten. And that was good enough wasn't it?

Well not quite. That bloody Mike Hargreaves told her that she needed to work harder and develop her very own signature moves, and then, oh yes, then; she might challenge the best in the world on her own terms.

She did, and she did!!!

And that Robert Redford, look alike, could do and think what he liked...she was hot to trot.

A LITTLE WHILE LATER!

The Noosa beaches were littered with young people all trying to get a 48-hour suntan before going back to- well frankly, it was mainly Melbourne.   They were slathered with coconut oil... Boy will they pay for it in later years, their eyes hopefully protected by fake Gucci sun glasses. On and around the beach there were mirrors all over the place.

Mike sauntered on to the beach and checked himself out in just about every pesky mirror. Pull the stomach in and flex the pecs. Oh yeah that made him look at least 10 years younger. He also stared at the girls' sun glasses...

Well they looked like a mirror.... Don't you get it!

The girls giggled at him without realising that he only had eyes for just one person! ---- Yup that's what I mean, he was deeply impressed with his own image.

He eventually saw Melinda and ran over to her and told her, with some pride, that they had made the team to compete in Nagano at the next

Olympics. He then smiled his Colgate grin and told her that she should be proud of their achievements.

What he really meant was that he secretly accepted most of the credit for Mellie's success------ Well not even secretly really...Good God everyone at the gym knew how enormously impressed he was with his own reflected glory.

 Actually, he was going over as an advisor, and nothing else; having never once been on the slopes in his life.   It was far too dangerous for someone of his Charles Atlas type physique.

A number of her friends came over and told her how lucky she was. "Mellie you've really got it made, babe." Everyone called her Mellie, and Mellie rather liked it,   she felt like a well toasted and utterly contented Mellie.

Her parents phoned to tell her how proud they were of her, and added, that she really should look after herself... "Darling you can be a bit scruffy at times,   course it's not your fault, you've always been a bit like that haven't you"!

The sports Minister also contacted her and told her that he would be thinking of her. Of course, he would! Dirty sod had tried to fondle her bum last time they met. Anyway he told her that he expected that she should do as well as she possibly could. Have a good time and try not to get too pissed at the Olympic village after the first round of her event.

The obvious implication being, that he didn't really expect her to make the second round... Well bugger him! All of a sudden, it made her gird her loins, whatever they were. She would show the doubting swine. Loins would be oiled and well and truly girded. You bet your sweet bippy they would....

A FEW MORE MONTHS GO BY.

NAGANO, WINTER OLYMPIC GAMES.

Having left the, almost maternal, warmth and comfort, of the Queensland beaches well and truly behind her. Mellie was on her way. She found herself at the snow fields of Hakuba village in Nagano on the banks of the lovely Chikuma River! Utterly enchanting, but unbelievably frigid.   Not a place for brass monkeys thought she, oh dear me no. But then she remembered that she had competed there before and recalled the snow Monkeys of Jigokudani. They, sensibly relaxed by bathing in the warm waters of the lake. How very smart they were, and apparently still are. They happily do it by completely ignoring their many admirers. A good lesson to be learnt!

She checked into her allotted room at Tsugaike Kogen resort and immediately tried to catch up with the few people she knew.   They all looked as if they'd only just left school and needed a letter from their mum to stay out at night.

She had a lot to learn about the new ascending youth....... However they were pleasant enough and Millie ended up acting, rather like a den mother. All those Sandra Dee movies of the seventies had a lot to answer for. However, she wasn't there to make friends, she had only one thought in mind and that was to get to the snow fields outside the city and practice, practice, practice.

Nothing else mattered.

It seemed to Mellie that wherever you go in the world, if there is natural snow or ice, whether it be, Japan, China or even South America, you always seemed to hear German oompah music, it's pretty much the law. Mellie rather liked it. Somehow it made her feel safer. But the food was a different matter. Who the hell eats seaweed - at least on purpose?

The resort was a bus trip of nearly six miles from the ski fields and then you had to go up by T bar to the top of the starting bay. Always freezing and almost impossible to hear anything. Everyone developed a sort of sixth sense and ultimately a sign language because the noise was so intense.

Mellie had already gone to the gym and gone through her stretching routine. All the girls did it. It was always amazing to Mellie just how quiet the gym was, just a few grunts and the occasional fart; but their workouts were absolutely paramount, and Mellie felt that her success, and even life and limb depended on them! Then of course breakfast, without a hint of seaweed, and onto the bus that would take them to the mountain.

Everything had to be checked. The right clothes, competition goggles and of course skis. Nothing could be forgotten. Once at the mountain face it was too late! Mellie smiled at the other girls who were chatting about the really important thing going on in the world, music and films that was pretty much it. Nobody ever seemed to talk about the day's practice, or what was to come. The only exception to this was Collette. She was one of the most beautiful girls that Mellie had ever seen, quite tall with the most superb, gymnastic physique she had ever come across. She hailed from the Nordic part of

Saskatchewan and gloried in the age of fifteen years. She had been skiing since she was five years old. Had never had an accident, not even a sprained ankle. She was absolutely brilliant, completely fearless and totally certain of her future. She was the quintessence of ten-foot-tall and bullet proof, she was also utterly delightful with a charm that seemed infectious to everyone.

Exactly two days prior to the competition you have to book as much time as you possibly can on the practice runs. The Japanese ensured that there were at least four of them. Each one laid out with typical Japanese efficiency. A good start thought Millie! Each of the girls had a particular favourite move, but the aerials were mandatory and the most important ones

Mellie had perfected her single twisting triple flip and her reputation was developing amongst the other girls, who, it must be said, were trying new moves all the time. Somersaults and even back flips were becoming part and parcel of the Winter Olympics for females. Mellie was quite happy with her routine but decided to give it a go just one more time. She had always been a girl to give more than 100 percent. She would never die wondering!

She joined the other girls on the bus that would take them back to the Kogen resort. Most of the girls were chatting quietly amongst themselves. With the exception of Collette who talked nonstop on her mobile phone to, well, it sounded like a boyfriend in Canada. She literally never stopped chatting, laughing and giggling all at the same time. She was an utter joy and continued to charm everyone.

Each day was the same routine; exactitude was what made them the champions, they were. If anything, toiling even harder. There was no going back, it was do or die. Nothing else mattered.

The very day before the competition started. Most of the girls admitted that they were more than somewhat nervous. They had all received messages from families, friends and even some heads of state.

 Big deal, thought Mellie who, apart from an old girlfriend on the Gold coast who sent her a message via her mobile phone, received no messages.   Actually she found out later that she had had quite a few messages wishing her good luck but they were mysteriously sent to a different resort. Oh well, who cares, thought Mellie; whilst in fact she did care. Rather a lot. It did however make Mellie even more determined. She would show them!!!

PRACTICE DAY

Mellie was one of the last to mount the steps that took them to the READY - GO point.

 What actually happened was this. The starter would count down. 5.4.3.2.1. And then tap them on the shoulder. In many cases, because it was so windy at the top, you couldn't always hear clearly. But you could always feel the strong tap on the shoulder.

As usual Collette was talking on her mobile phone to whomever! She obviously turned it off when the starter called her to READY. She walked forward, turned and gave Mellie a huge wink and an utterly radiant smile, then, after the tap she took off....

 No one will ever know exactly what happened. But in the midst of her backward flip she missed her vital footing and landed on her head.

She was dead by the time she slid slowly and gracefully down to the bottom of the run.

There was talk of cancelling the games—it came down to a sort of democratic vote. This had happened before, but very, very rarely. Everyone was utterly shattered.

Amazingly enough, after Collette's parents had flown over from Canada. They very bravely and stoically said that Collette would want the games to continue. And they insisted on being there amongst her friends. Collette was very simply a special person.

Some of the girls felt a bit uneasy but her folks turned out to be such smashing people that they were quickly accepted into the group. Comments like, "Well you can see where she got it from" abounded.

Mike, rather amazingly didn't want it to go ahead, Mellie didn't know why. Mellie was completely lost. Her head was in an amazing cloud filled kerfuffle. Mike told her that she should make up her own mind. She was going to do that anyway, whatever anyone said. It was odd, but she never found out why Mike was so against the event continuing and, in the end, it made no difference. But it was just one more cog in her decision making process…

The following day the girls all met at breakfast and, after an impromptu meeting amongst themselves, came to the decision that, with the approval of the management, they would carry on with the games, almost as scheduled. Mellie wasn't so sure but she didn't feel strong enough to argue, Mike still seemed even less keen to continue, and Mellie had no idea why…but it gave her an uneasy feel in her gut!

THE OPENING CEREMONY.

The start of the Games was pretty much taken up with the usual pomp and showmanship. Millie had little interest in that part of the Olympics.   Still one had to admit that it was pretty spectacular.   She admired the typical efficiency of the Japanese. However, her mind was elsewhere!!!!!

MONDAY MORNING.

The men opened the competition with the standard two acrobatic jumps demanded in the qualifying round. Later of course the twelve finalists perform two more jumps of varying difficulty. It went on all day until the inevitable and ultimate winner was declared.

Big deal—

Mellie didn't think he was all that good. But eventually he had a gold medal round his neck----and you can't argue with the colour of the metal...

TUESDAY MORNING.

Five clock in the morning. Mellie had hardly slept
a wink all night.

 It was her time. All the hard work over the years
came to this. It was like yearning for a meal that
you had only heard of or read about. And now,
here it was plonked in front of her, I dunno, I'm
not that sure I'm hungry anymore.

She showered and got ready for the day—Mellie
tried to remind herself that her whole life had
been in readiness for this one event. She brushed
her teeth with a little more vigour than usual. It
didn't help one tiny iota! A really big sigh, and
then get dressed and face the Mellie world.

She saw Mike, who almost completely ignored
her, why she thought? Somehow, she felt that it
had something to do with Collette. But how
could it?

Mellie's brain clicked into place----- She knew
what she had to do. She simply had to go ahead
with it. No. No more, absolutely. No more......

Mellie knew now that she had to make a monumental decision. This was the strangest epiphany she had ever felt, but she knew that she couldn't ignore it. She fully realised that a lot of people would be horribly disappointed, including family and dear friends.

Equally, she knew it was the right thing, for her, at least. Of that she felt very, very certain.

Mellie felt a dreadful calmness flood over psyche.

 Just do it and get the hell away.

WOMENS FREESTYLE SKIING

Mellie was the eighth competitor in line. There were two German girls a Norwegian, two Swedes and the American lasses.

She took an enormous gulp of Japanese mountain air then got to her place and boldly went over to the starter official and very clearly said. "I've decided not to take my place". He looked at her as though she had rather amusingly told him that World War Three had just begun. He started to argue and pointed out all the people she would be forsaking.

 Mellie just smiled at him and shook her head, the dumfounded official immediately got on the two-way to Mike.

Mellie could only just here what Mike said. It was very crackly but audible..."Tell that blood—crackle, crackle--- that —crackle, crackle —f-- k — crackle, crackle to get her crackle, crackle arse onto the crackle—crackle -- skis or she will never crackle- crackle again.

Mellie did strap her skis on again. She waved to all the girls, who were staring at her; most of them with mixed emotions. Two of the girls smiled and nodded. A lot more just shook their heads and got back to the reason they were there. Fair enough.

Mellie very slowly made her way down to the bottom of the normal ski run, knowing that she would never again be in a competition. That'll do me just fine! As she came round one of the bends on the downhill slalom a slow but almost beatific smile washed over her face.

Yes, oh yes!

SABAH THE POOCH

A very, very good friend.

It was about two o'clock in the morning when the healthy Cross breed bitch started to feel the inevitable rumbling in her belly. She was part Blue Heeler, part German shepherd with a fair amount of dingo in her. She rather proudly told all the other dogs of her native heritage. Well partly pride, and a fair bit of bravado, just to keep the others a little bit wary. It pays to keep all your four paws on the ground when you're by yourself!

It was going to happen shortly. This was her second litter, and two o'clock in the morning was a good time to whelp, it was as cool as it was ever going to be. She had found a safe place to bring her progeny into the world. She was entirely by herself with the exception of her elder sister who was quietly keeping guard, in, and around the area. Woe betide any other dog that came within cooee of her favourite sister.

She eventually produced five pups, Woof 1, Woof 2, Woof 3 and of course Woof 4. The last pup took longer to enter the world, and was, rather unsurprisingly, yet inevitably, given the name Woof 5. Woof 5 heard his mother's sister [You know, the bolshie watch dog] say that he was the runt. It made him feel pretty special. He told all his brothers and sisters that he was the only one. He didn't quite know why that made him so unique, but he knew it was good... Special he was and special he would always remain. Damn right he would.

His brothers and sisters were already suckling at mum's milk bar, although, by the time he got there, most of the good stuff had already been taken by his siblings. Still it wasn't too bad, Mum gave him a special lick and he settled down to puppy nap and dream with his mates.

All the guys very quickly got used to the sound of their own particular bark. Each one of them could tell if Mum wanted them, or, if there was danger around in any shape or form, and Mum was able to identify each pup by the slightest noise. Course Mum was pretty darn clever like that. Way to go Mum!!

Life was pretty simple really! It consisted of rousting about with the rest of the guys. Good food, that's if he could get it. Then fun, fun, fun. And course plenty of sleep…Oh yes Boyo, life was OK. They lived judiciously and simply on the edge of a rather pleasant town in Western Australia called Broome. It turned out that people up there didn't so much as buy pups. No way, they sort of adopted them. And that's what happened to Woof 5.

One day, he was watching the world go by and thinking about food. Well of course he was, Mum's udder had completely stopped producing milk! So, things were getting to be pretty desperate. Woof 5 hadn't understood that his mother had died. She had eaten something that was poisonous to her system. So, she made the instinctive decision to go away to end her life. She naturally understood that her milk would destroy her family, so she found a quiet place to end her time on earth without harming her offspring.

Woof 5 didn't get any of this. How could he, he was only a few weeks old? But food takes over as a priority very quickly when you're starving.

THE BOYS ENTER HIS LIFE

David and Bud [short for Bruno] were throwing stones across the road to see who the best shot. It was Dave, of course, it was always Dave. He was older and really good at it and he hit the pesky rusty tin at least six times before they caught sight of Woof 5. They ran over to him to make sure he was OK...He was. He actually thought it was pretty good game. The boys decided that woof looked a bit hungry so gave him part of the sandwiches they had brought with them. Woof immediately ate the food and gave a satisfied bark and a bit of a lick to the boys.

That's how friendships start in his world.

Woof decided to keep the boys! That was it. Simple really, pals forever. Woof was a puppy that liked to play and lick. Licking was instinctive to him, something to do with the need for body salt; that, and of course, recognition. Woof didn't know what the guys were talking about, he simply enjoyed leaping about and having a good old time. The boys adored him. He joined them wherever they went. Even when Dave went to soccer training.

Woof thought that soccer was the most boring game he had ever seen. Of course he hadn't actually seen any other games, but you get the picture. Whenever Dave seemed to do something pretty darn good, everyone clapped and cheered, and of course Woof scampered over to Dave to give him a celebratory lick and a really good bark. But there always seemed to be some guys amongst the other players who didn't really understand his almost insane puppy joy at Dave's success, in fact he was so full of canine cocker hoopery that he started to cough, so much so, that he couldn't seem to stop.

Henry Sandos was the father of Dave and Bud. Henry was part aboriginal and part Japanese, as were so many in that area of the world. He had just got back from a trip on one of the last Pearl luggers to still operate in Broome. He was an undersea diver, and a damn good one at that. But he was aware that technology was taking over the pearling industry and he wouldn't have the same job for very much longer. He loved getting back to port to spend a few days with his lovely wife and the boys.

Henry arrived at the soccer field in time to watch Dave score a magnificent goal right into the high left-hand corner of the net. He was proud of the lads and joined the rest of the supporters as they patted him on the back. "Yes, matey that goal won the match, that's for sure". He knew that it was important to support the boys in whatever sport they chose, but he was an Aussie Rules man! Always had been, always would be, and that's all there was to it!

This was the first time Henry had had any contact with Woof. He was running around the field having a great old time but stopping as he fell to the ground when the coughing became too much for him. Henry listened to the pup and instinctively realised that something was seriously wrong with him. His coughing seemed to come from the very heart of the animal. It turned out that he was ominously correct about that!

He waited until the game was over before telling the boys of his concern. He knew how important friendship with a dog could be. Whilst he was growing up, his whole area was surrounded by dogs, they were used as hunting animals and guard dogs, but of course they also became pals. Henry was a very powerful man but he gently picked up the pup and took him over to his car. As he cradled Woof in his arms, he quickly realised how undernourished the dog was.

The boys were extremely upset because they had both been looking after Woof and they knew that he had been getting plenty of good food and milk, they also kept him as clean as they possibly could. Henry explained to the boys that it was in no way their fault; Woof had been very well looked after but something had gone seriously wrong with the digestive system of the animal.

Henry told Dave and Bud that he knew the local vet as he used to play basketball with him a few years ago. Henry tried to tell the boys, as gently as he could, that it was very serious. He explained to them that vets often had to work long hours and he might still be at the clinic. Luckily, Marcus the vet, was still at the hospital. He brought them through to the examination room. It was all stainless steel and smelled of antiseptic wash. He told the guys to be very quiet so he could listen very carefully through his stethoscope to the laboured breathing of the pet. It didn't take long before Marcus realised that he would have to tell all the three fellas, and of course Woof that he was almost certain that the dog had serious heart worms. Woof could sense that the boys were very upset so he gave them his really best friendship lick. Marcus said, rather sternly, that licking wasn't a good idea and Woof really should go into quarantine immediately.

Woof thought that was OK by him, so long as the food was good! The Vet took Henry into his small office and explained the simple truth to him. In reality he wasn't able to treat the dog in an effective way in Broome because he just didn't have the right drugs, but he did have an idea. That very night he was going to drive down to Perth to attend a seminar that was run by Professor Dressnau who, by lucky coincidence, was an accepted expert in the treatment of heart worm victims, amongst many other things. It was literally the dogs' only chance. He couldn't think of an alternative. He looked at Henry and said that he understood how upset he was, but the boys, in particular, would be pretty devastated.

He had always dreaded telling young people the bad news that occasionally goes with looking after animals. The Veterinary course at UNI prepares you for pretty much everything you can imagine as far as the treatment of animals goes, but explaining the inevitable to kids was not part of the curriculum. And he found over the years, that he had developed a tough exterior that wasn't always at one with his personality. The best way is always to tell the absolute truth and leave explanations to time and experience to become the honest healers. Henry left the vet's office but asked Marcus to keep him in the loop as far as Woof's health was concerned. He thanked the vet for all the trouble he was prepared to go to.

Marcus had to prepare Woof for his rather long journey to Perth. He would have to be sedated for the twenty-hour journey to the West Australian capital. In fact, for quite a long time he would need to be as relaxed as possible. It would become a specific part of the treatment, but more of that later.

Henry brought the boys into the surgery. It was by way of saying goodbye, the lads didn't really understand and they were very, very sad when they saw Woof almost asleep in the basket. Woof, who really is the hero of this tale, summoned enough strength to give them both a really good bark and to each of the boys an extra special lick. The lads were unhappy for quite a while. They couldn't, of course, know that Woof had inadvertently given them a love of animals that lasted both of them forever.

Marcus made sure that Woof was comfy in the back of his Landrover, and then took off on the long, predominantly straight road, to Perth. They arrived at Freemantle on Friday night. Marcus immediately took Woof to Professor Dressnau's surgery on the outskirts of Freemantle. The old man had seen hundreds of cases like Woof over the years and insisted on starting treatment immediately. It really was a matter of life and death.

Marcus understood that the drugs were arsenic based and would need to be administered very carefully, especially over the first few days. Woof could not be allowed to get excited during the treatment. Hence it was imperative that that he was kept mildly sedated for the next six weeks. Woof didn't really mind; the food was pretty good. But he had some really odd dreams, some of them were actually scary and he wished he could tell his Mum all about them. The other guys in the place were OK but they seemed to kip most of the time. How very weird he thought. Then he went straight back to sleep.

After six weeks the old Professor said he was coming along nicely, they'd gotten rid of most of the grotty worms in his system, then, would you believe it, they treated him all over again. To eradicate any eggs that might still be in his system. To be sure, to be sure!

Marcus had long since gone back up to Broome, and he was able to give the boys the good news that Woof was coming along very well. He didn't however, tell them that he wouldn't be coming back up to Broome. He was going to be a Perth dog from now on. With his treatment successfully completed, Woof was able to get off the pesky sedatives and have a good old chat with some of the other dogs. Quite a few of them were older than him but none of them had his exotic background.

 Woof told them all about his family and, in particular about the boys. The other animals seemed pretty darned impressed. So he also told them that his aunt (you remember the bolshie one) was over eight feet tall and had once attacked a ferocious tiger, whatever that was. Woof had developed a healthy disregard for reality and could have spent quite a lot more time with his new mates, but his life was destined for a much different path.

Pretty darned exciting too!

Woof was given a complete clean bill of health and was sent to a new place called RSPCA. He decided that he would check it out. See what it was like. Was the food OK? What were the other guys like? Very important if you were a dog like Woof.

One of the really odd things that happened was that they gave him a new name Sabah. It was alright I suppose, thought the boyo. But he always felt more like a woof than a Sabah. But the name Sabah seemed to bring the good food so, OK he would go along with it. He was getting stronger and stronger as the days went by.

The one thing Sabah didn't like was living in this thing they called a cage. He thoroughly disapproved of the damn things and told the people who ran the place. But they didn't seem to understand his point of view. How very odd!!! Still it wouldn't be for long.

On a regular basis other dogs were led out of the place, never to be seen again. Sabah was a little bit concerned, but of course he had complete faith in the system.

Yeah right!

On a sunny Thursday afternoon at approximately half hour before dinner time. A group of people came in to the RSPCA. They seemed very ordinary to Woof, sorry Sabah. They walked up and down and passed most of the cages and talked to a few of his new mates. They appeared to be to be checking them out. Sabah cast a withering eye over the group and then chose a rather scruffy looking fella with filthy shoes. His name was Jonathon and they had a really good chat.

Sabah felt that he was OK, so he gave him a really good licking and a friendly bark, and that was it. Second time in his life, mates forever, again!

Goodbye RSPCA.

Hello Perth.

A FLASH OF LIGHT WILL BRING IT ALL
TOGETHER.

Jonathon had decided to try to make it as a
photographer. He started by travelling all the
way to Western Australia. A new state, a new
start. He literally had no training, no real
qualifications, only a special eye for the sense of
light that always seemed so very vital to him. If
that's all you've got then take a deep breath and
go for it. It seemed like the best idea he'd had
for a long time.

He purchased a Nikon FMX2 with a 50 mm lens,
the best camera that he could afford at the time.
He had read that to be an independent
photographer was the obvious way to go, or so
he thought. Jonathon had a lot to learn about
photo- journalism! He would present himself to
all the major newspapers in the State and see
what happened.   It took less than a month
before he realised how complicated it was going
to be.

Jonathon was nearly out of money and now, of
course, he had a dog to look after, He found a
part time job washing cars and doing

maintenance work for a car hire firm. They also let him sleep in the back shed, with, of course Sabah. Actually, Sabah proved to be a pretty good watch dog. More bark than bite, but nobody else knew that. So, bring on the Pal meaty bites!

Jonathon was a naturally gifted photographer, but it seemed to him that just about everyone else had a similar talent. He very quickly realised that there were dozens of other photojournalists who yearned to make a living with a camera in hand. He had yet to learn how to look at life through a camera lens!!!

Jonathon had arbitrarily decided to concentrate on shooting quirky buildings and sport meetings, nothing else. That was it. Like that famous piece of plastic, he never left home without his camera. It became a part of him. A few of the people he hung with thought him a little peculiar. Well maybe he was, but he had learnt to trust his instincts, right or wrong.

It was at least fourteen months before he got his first major break. He and Sabah were in a place called Kalgoorlie, walking around looking for something to capture on film. It was July and the sun was setting on Hay Street. The time was approximately four thirty in the afternoon. The light still shone very brightly and conveniently on all of the small workers cottages. Except for one, why, he didn't know. But he immediately recognised that it was special. It somehow captured the charm and uniqueness of the isolated gold mining city.

That was it.

The photograph made headlines in the West Australian paper and, three days later, amazingly enough, it was also picked up by a number of national papers. So, Jonathon, and his camera, and his dog, were on their way. Not a bad way to look at life, through that ubiquitous 300mm telephoto lens. Sabah became his best mate as well as his good luck token, they were almost inseparable, and somehow they relied upon each other. Jonathon took Sabah with him wherever he went. They completed each other...neither one being more important than the other, mates!

A FEW WEEKS LATER.

Friday afternoon in September, it wasn't really that hot, in fact it had been raining and was getting a bit muggy, and Jonathon hadn't really had a prosperous time of late. But success could be just around the corner. As usual he had Sabah with him. Jonathon scanned the sites along Parmelia Road. The sun was just shining through onto one of the ubiquitous glass buildings that made up the city centre of Perth. It was perfect, a shot of a life time. He relaxed everything, including the leash he had on Sabah, took a deep breath, pointed his camera and captured the most perfect picture he'd ever taken. Just three seconds later and it would have been nothing, he got at least ten shots before the sun light changed. It was as special as you could get!

Jonathon looked round for Sabah to share his joy. He couldn't see him, Friday afternoon in Perth and the traffic was horrendous. Sabah had actually only gone twenty metres along the pavement, and would you believe it, he saw one of his mates from the RSPCA, he barked quite loudly, but his pal obviously didn't hear him over the noise of the traffic. No matter, he would go over to see him. He was just about to leap across the busy road when this person grabbed hold of him with amazing speed and strength and held on to him.

A few moments later Jonathon ran over with panic in his eyes. "Thank you so much, I could see you reach out for Sabah, I think you saved his life, we're both very grateful to you, he's my best mate"

Sabah gave the very attractive lady a special bark of thanks and a bit of a lick. Then both he and Jonathon walked away, back to the glass building. Jonathon tried to recapture the shot, but the moment had passed, that's the way it is with photography.

He started to walk back to his parked car but could feel Sabah pulling on his leash. Sabah had turned to look back at the lady, he sort of nodded and barked once more. She waved back and smiled.

Mellie was that sort of person.

This will be a new beginning…

PLEASE DON'T EXPLAIN.

JEREMY LOWLEY

She was a woman of great natural ability.

However her maths were appalling.

Her written English was worse.

Geography - who needs it – Mesopotamia? Who cares? Apart from the Mesopotamians of course.

But when she planted seeds, they all knew that they stood a very good chance of becoming the ripest, most delicious vegetables or fruit you've ever tasted in your life.

Her name was Dorothy [Dotty] and, frankly she could be a pain in the bum.   But boy oh boy---- She never needed to learn anything from books about botany, or plant life, or life for that matter.

Somehow, she naturally knew everything that was important.

Dotty was born with the most compelling understanding of all things organic; yet she lived in one of the hottest parts of Australia during the summer months   and, of course, frigidly cold in the winter season.

Not an impossible place to survive - but it was a close thing.

Yet she managed to feed her tiny family with the ludicrously small amount of water that was left over to her, after bathing, washing clothes and of course, general washing up. Nothing was ever thrown away.

First rule: Nothing to be wasted. It was a sin of the first order.

Second rule: Water is more valuable than gold.

Third rule: There isn't one. Life was too difficult to worry about trivial things.

Dotty taught me everything I know about gardens and, all things allied. I learnt the value of the quality of earth, very little grows in hot dry sand. How shade could be your best friend. The simple way to take cuttings, and of course, turning them into viable plants that actually cost virtually nothing. Good sensible economics, and practical too.

But more than anything else, she imbued me with a love of nature that has stayed with me forever. In simple terms she was my teacher, I owe her. Regrettably, I didn't recognise it at the time.

She suffered from two problems as far as I was concerned.

Firstly. She simply couldn't tell the truth.   A situation that allowed her to say anything she liked, and rarely, if ever, to accept any of the consequences.

Secondly. She reached the stage where she could look people in the eye, smile sweetly, and deny absolutely everything.

 Her memory was so reliably appalling that she frequently forgot what she had so adamantly insisted upon only moments earlier.

This had the most amazing effect on various members of society. For instance:

A.   Her poor bedraggled husband

B.   Her very confused children---

C.   The Inland Revenue department, loveless swine that they are

D.   Quite a number of her paying customers.

Not really a good plan when, money in the pocket was the issue.

However, as I came to know Dotty better, I began to realise that she suffered from a genuine case of convenient memory loss, very useful, if you can sweetly swear blind that you never said   anything of the sort and actually believe it.

That day was just such a day.

A valued customer had ordered, and paid for, a large number of plants. Approximately one hundred and fifty dollars' worth. Quite a tidy sum of money in the good old days.

 A week and a half later, the poor benighted customer arrived, fully expecting to take his plants home in a recently hired trailer. Not an unreasonable action you would think...

I was helping out at the nursery when the guy and his family showed up. He smilingly asked if his plants were ready for loading and despatching.

I won't easily forget the sweet beatific smile that came over Dotty's face. It was, part bewilderment and a larger part, genuine amazement.

She smilingly asked "And who are you?" The customer, fairly reasonably convinced that, this was a jolly good joke on Dotty's part said. "You know the plants I ordered, and paid for last week".

 Dotty looked him straight in the face and uttered. "I've never seen you in my life before! Who are you? What are you doing here? What is your name?"

Now names in her business were a little bit like the botanical name for plants. You know, all that Latin stuff, very important to those who cared, but, to the Dotties of this world, vastly overrated. And anyway she kept no record of her transactions, so it never occurred to her to actually write anything down. It was all in her computer like brain.........OOPS!

I believe that a minor botanical World War Three was averted when the husband of Dotty ran out and saved the day by slightly hysterically screaming: "They're here, they're here, they're bloody here!"

Dotty, quite reasonably and sweetly said, "Oh those plants. Yes they've been here for quite a while. I thought you'd forgotten all about them. I was just about to sell them." She spoke as she walked away in a cloud of innocent exactitude.

Leaving:

1. A bewildered customer, well at least he got his plants.

2. A very confused husband.

3. A recent son-in-law very keen to find the nearest pub.

All of us trying to work out what had just happened.

The simple moral to the tale is this. The customer got his plants. The Dotty got a happy customer. The husband got his wife and I got a glass of cold lager...

But most important of all. Dotty produced the sweetest tomatoes I've ever tasted in my life.

So who cares about some unpaid tax bills?

JEREMY LOWLEY

Chapter one.

Helen leapt out of bed with her customary enthusiasm. She had always been a hale and hearty girl, so being a pound or two overweight had never bothered her, she could easily burn that off, so it didn't really matter… did it!!

She completed her exercise routine with the bland enthusiasm that ennui tends to create.

Helen was quite aware that her life was soon to change in a way that she would have very little control of. Not exactly her favourite direction, but, well let's see which cards she is dealt!

She arrived at the newly opened university teaching school, in Richmond, NSW, and decided to embrace just about every aspect of UNI life on offer, including, of course, joining the netball team.

All the girls were doing it, so why not!

The notice board suggested that all enthusiastic newcomers should be available for trials the following Friday afternoon at approximately 3 o'clock, 'on the very dot.'

Helen decided to have a go. She'd show them what an Aussie country girl could do.

She was determined to be accepted as 'one of the girls.' Right up until the moment when she overheard the team vice-captain describe her as, "That new chubby lass with the bulging biceps. Maybe she should try out for the girls wrestling team, they're definitely looking for the slightly more 'butch' type of girl."

From that day on, Helen developed the exercise routine that would become her early morning 'way of life' for ever, and a day.

She also developed a loathing for the very vice-captain she overheard, to the point where she actually considered doing her harm, not a lot of course, but enough to annoy the living daylights out of her, and maybe scare her somewhat... She didn't actually do anything,   but it crossed her mind!

It also encouraged her to maintain her ambition to become a head mistress, whilst accepting the reality that she would need to attain teacher status first.   However, there was no doubting in her mind that the eventual top job was her only goal.

In many ways the netball vice-captain had inadvertently pushed her to become the resolute and determined woman that she had every intention of developing into.   A fit, strong, slightly masculine, academic woman of the world, with just the tiniest chip on both of her shoulders.

It was during her first term at UNI, that she ran into Andrew Piermont. Andy, [he resented being called Andrew. Andy had a much more Aussie twang to it], was one of the darlings of the teaching college.

Andy could do no wrong! He was blessed with a physique that didn't really need much exercise to maintain what DNA had so graciously given him at birth, including a chiselled feature face that was just this side of effeminate. Everything came ludicrously easily to Andy. He was consecrated with the adoration that only the 'silver spooned' could appreciate….whether it be academic degrees, or compliant girlfriends.

Even the bloody footballs seemed to come to rest at his feet… so goal scoring was easy. You do get it don't you? Well of course you do!!

The real point being that he was such a charmer that he knew no rancour from anyone, just adoring fans!

Count Helen amongst this throng.

They met due to a mutual fascination with photography. The course was not an actual part of the university degree curriculum, just an in-house interest.

Helen had acquired her father's old Canon SLR camera, an excellent unit which, for all its fifteen years of age, was almost like new. Her Pop discovered that it was far too complicated to operate the damn thing. Hence, he was quite pleased to relay it on to his beloved daughter. Complete with the rest of the kit including the inevitable telephoto lens and the wide-angle unit. All equally unused.

Why he purchased the thing in the first place was never really explained, so Helen, who enjoyed the love of her Father, never asked him …. a wise girl!

Helen gradually discovered that she was naturally talented and blessed, with an artistic way of viewing her subjects that made her stand out in the class…Her artistic ability was in fact how Andy and she got together.

Andy never really had to worry about anything in life, he simply mentioned to the head of the family that he needed a camera and his dear old Uncle Harry, who frequently travelled to the eastern parts of the world, purchased, and then presented him with a brand new digital system camera kit, from jolly old Japan.

It was, of course, the most expensive camera on the market, every lens that was manufactured was included in the kit, also a range of filters to fit every occasion… whether you needed them or not.

All explained in a complete, and beautifully detailed instruction booklet… In fluent, incomprehensible Japanese, of course.

Once the winter weather had waved goodbye to Sydney and the surrounds, to be gradually followed by the inevitable warmth of spring, the photography class [they called themselves the 'clickers'] decided to embark on a trip into the beguiling Blue Mountains in the hinterlands of Sydney.

They had all of them been there before and been enthralled by the raw beauty of their surroundings.   But this photographic trip was new to all of them…. They were by themselves. It was rather exciting!!

Each one of them wanted to snap the enigmatic Three Sisters from every view that was safely available…and at least two angles, that were decidedly unsafe. It all went rather swimmingly.

Andy ensured that he had commandeered the largest tent available… actually, it was one that could easily house four enthusiastic camping photographers, including all their kit. A wonderfully spacious and waterproof tent. Nothing dubious there… yet!!

Andy arranged for Helen to share the tent with him and two other enthusiastic photographers… on an entirely platonic basis, of course!

They all got on rather well.   Helen proved to be an excellent arbiter of scenic choice. It turned out that she had a natural ability to sense unusual aspects of the famous sisters, so rather naturally, she became the leader of the group.

Ultimately it proved to be a magnificent forty-eight-hour trip. They took an enormous number of truly spectacular shots, having clambered up and down the inevitable rock faces. No one got hurt, apart from a few scrapes and bruises… but dude…they were exhausted!

They got back to the camp site, to be told, rather surprisingly, that David and Sally, their fellow tent dwellers, had decided to go back to Sydney for a family get-together…odd really, they hadn't mentioned it before…Ah well can't be helped.

Helen blithely sorted it out by saying, it didn't bother her at all, and she simply wanted eight hours sleep… that is, after a bite to eat…naturally.

Andy had in fact produced a rare and inviting lunch…oddly enough, for just the two of them, comprising small tins of foie gras, equally small, but delicious portions of Tasmanian lobster, followed of course, by some excellent camembert cheese. Oh yes, and they quaffed three bottles of superb fruit driven Chianti wine.

They ate and drank, and laughed, and cried, whilst partying into the lonely night.

At approximately five o-clock in the morning, Helen awoke with the worst headache ever. In truth, this was the very first hangover in her relatively short life. She also realised, with embarrassing effect, that she was stark naked, if this wasn't shocking enough, she also recognised that she had shared the sleeping bag with dear old Andy, who was sleeping away with innocent abandonment.

Helen, armed herself with her trusty camera, and clicked away at everything in and around the tent, including the comatose Andy. She used every shot left in her well-handled Canon.

It was only later when she studied the prints that she spied all three of the empty Chianti bottles.

Oh, what a price she paid for those ruby red delicious wines.

Thirty-five days later she sat in the office of her dear friend and family physician, Doctor Gloria Berry, who knowingly smiled as she entered the clinic examination ward and told Helen the really good news, that is, that she had about seven and a half months prior to the birth of her child.

Helen stoically accepted the news and reminded herself that she still had exactly two and a half years before her final exams to complete her teacher's degree. Timing, as usual, was everything.

Her plans for a headmistress appointment would have to wait, but only in abeyance. Nothing was going to stop her ambitions.

As she left the clinic, she thought to herself, now for the difficult part, as she dialled on her mobile phone.

'Andy, do you remember those photos that turned out so incredibly? Well, I have some news for you'

Moving right along!

The wedding turned out to be rather a splendid affair. The two families, whist being socially miles apart, actually got on famously, Helen was enormously proud of her folks, particularly her father, He was charming, quite amusing, and was, in every way the supportive Dad she always knew he would be.   He actually smiled radiantly as he proudly escorted Helen down the aisle of the small church in Windsor.

Helen wore a lovely dress, which made no attempt to hide the very obvious baby bump that she carried so graciously down to her future husband.

They both said their I do's with a smile on their collective faces, and a warm glow in their hearts.

This was a marriage for ever!

Chapter two.

Eleven years later, as per usual, things had changed somewhat!

Helen gingerly opened the letter from the Education dept. She was in the shade of the jacaranda tree in her garden, but her fingers were slightly sweaty as she carefully unfurled the typed document,

The letter opened by saying:

Dear Mrs Piermont, etc, etc, etc, after due consideration, The private school's board is delighted to offer you.....rhubarb, rhubarb, rhubarb.   The rest didn't really matter, Helen knew exactly what the contents were......at last, an offer of a position as Assistant Headmistress in a small school on the outskirts of the QLD Gold Coast.

Oh boy, at last---all her dreams in one letter.

In reality, in just one sentence!!

Helen ran into the house and then straight to the bathroom, she slammed, and locked the door behind her, then squatted on the toilet seat as she tried to sort out her convoluted thoughts.

She needed to be alone!

The last ten years of her life had been… what's the phrase? Happily complicated, with occasional frustration…

Yes, well that's close enough.

Helen had always found the business of teaching very satisfying, and she adored being around children, but she was dedicated to the ambition, that teaching would never be the 'be all and end all' of her life. She practiced the patience that she knew was demanded of her.

In truth, the past decade had been fraught for just about everyone in both of their families.

For instance:

Over twenty-five years earlier The Piermonts had invested all the money they had into a business selling sporting equipment. They named it…The Good Sportz… their timing was immaculate… either that, or they cashed in on the greatest fluke ever. Whatever the reason, they amassed a fortune from the gymnasium they initially operated from. It was in the Sydney south west area and absolutely perfect.   Within a relatively short period of time they had opened two more stores in NSW and one on the Queensland Gold Coast… which seemed like a natural progression at the time…things were certainly beginning to hum as the northern state expanded.

Once the newlyweds had settled down to married life. The Piermont family offered Andrew [Helen refused to call him Andy] the choice to manage whichever store he fancied. He originally opted for the inner Sydney store.

Well he would wouldn't he! It was the biggest and easiest store to handle, likewise the most profitable one.   It was also close to his family, in particular his Father, who still came into the store, literally every day, armed with the best advice, when needed… and occasionally, when not needed!   Helen remembered, sometime later, that Andrew hadn't even discussed with her where they would live… it was simply assumed!

Of course, if the truth be told, it really suited Helen down to the ground… nevertheless, it was a very bright beacon to their future. Or so she believed!

Oddly enough it was the presence of his mother that was so important to Andrew. Mrs Piermont had always been a 'hoverer'. She, recklessly adoringly viewed her son with a similar attitude as the sun chooses to rise in the east, and then reliably sets in the west in a trustworthy position later in the day!

Both mothers and sons could easily share an affinity … when it suited them!!

Like nearly all mums she was well aware of Andrew's weaknesses, she genuinely felt that it was opportune to ignore them, with the vague assumption that, one day, he would grow up and stand on his own two feet.

The good mother never once in his adult life confronted her son.

However, in the meantime, it was becoming more and more obvious to all concerned, That Andy was falling into an abyss, in both his business life, but also, and more importantly, his marriage.

None of his friends or his family seemed to be able to help him, mainly because he refused to listen to them… least of all to Helen.

Over the years Helen began to recognise that Mrs Piermont and she were, in fact, very similar in both character and attitude. Actually, it was Mrs Piermont that initially recognised that Andy seemed to completely lose all the ambitions that he, so flamboyantly enjoyed, when first he attended university.

Was it his marital status, or just the simplicity of making an easy living, without really having to struggle, or worry about the creative process a new business demands. Who knows?

Sure, as hell Andy didn't!

In many ways the Piedmont family situation actually allowed Helen to concentrate on her own academic ambitions, and of course to take care of their only child's education.

Young Steven's start in life was taking on characteristics that would almost certainly take their toll in his later years.

It was decided, with the endorsement of the family, that he should be enrolled in the South Sydney, St Jasper's preparatory school, it seemed absolutely perfect, he settled in immediately and did quite well scholastically… not brilliantly, but well enough.

Helen found out later that Andrew had spent his early years at St Jasper's.   So, the choice was not exactly a coincidence.

And in no way hers!!

She quickly understood that her problems lay with Andrew's apathy. Of course, it didn't just happen overnight, in fact, over the years he allowed his family to decide just about everything involving their livelihood, [including both Helen's and Stephen's]. Not just where they lived, but holiday destinations, which car Andrew might drive etc, etc.

He simply allowed the family to pay for everything, which pretty much, gave them carte-blanche control over their entire life.

Whilst Andrew happily sailed through life, seemingly, without a care in the world. He never once questioned the rightness of the situation. Obviously, it suited Andrew down to the ground.

Helen however, increasingly realised that they had major lifestyle problems… but what to do about them?

Andrew, whilst surrounded by very fit and athletic people from the sporting world, had physically, and, in some ways emotionally, let himself go. He so easily lost whatever discipline he once had. His, naturally slim and robust physique had disappeared, replaced by a beer gut, exacerbated by the fact that he didn't drink beer.

So, what!!

No one told him, certainly not his parents, and definitely not Helen, maybe it was easier that way.

Both Andrew and Helen adopted an attitude to young Stephen's livelihood that was becoming almost ludicrous. They both fussed over situations that really didn't need all the hullabaloo. In fact, Stephen was turning into a very independent young lad. He resented all the 'hoo-ha.' The Piedmonts recognised that he had adopted his mother's stoicism. A great quality when handled with loving care. But a pain in the neck if allowed to get out of hand!

It was the 22nd of January. Helen, Andy, and Stephen were on their annual Christmas holidays in Hobart, Tasmania.

And, in simple terms, they were bored to tears. It certainly wasn't poor old Tasmania's fault. This was their first time in the lonesome state. And they had found it a remarkably beautiful and welcoming place. Naturally they fell in love with the wondrous island, so cool and lush! Especially compared to Sydney at Christmas time. Unfortunately, the city of Hobart proved to be the only thing that inspired love.

Whilst both Andy and Helen still had a great deal of fondness for one another, their love was more like brotherly affection than romance.

Love had drifted like the morning tide, rarely to be seen again!

The intimate side of their marriage had slowly disintegrated over the years. Naturally, of course, neither of them discussed it. Like so many problems. It just, sort of dwindled. Sad really.

On the last day of their holiday Helen, as usual, was organising their return to Sydney. Young Stephen was looking forward to catching up with his mates. Tasmania was alright, but come on, nothing compared with the cafes of Sydney playing Dungeons and Dragons with his school pals.

Helen looked around and realised that she hadn't seen Andy for a while, she wasn't really worried. Of late, he frequently took off for a short time, presumably to be by himself. An hour passed with no sign of him. Helen was becoming slightly concerned; this wasn't like him. For all his weaknesses, Andy wasn't a thoughtless man, just cluelessly unaware!

They had hired a boat so the whole family could go fishing, it was moored at the local jetty. In truth, it had never once been used!

Helen ran down to the pier; the boat was still tied up, from a distance she could hear Andrew's voice. He seemed to be talking to someone. Who on earth could it be?

Helen never really had any doubts about Andrew, he was a very simple soul deep down, and still, she was very confused. She crept up to the boat and peeped through the port hole.   He was having a blazing row with someone but who? And why? And over what? There was no one else in the boat.

Andy was half shouting half sobbing at his invisible antagonist, but in reality, only at his own reflection in the mirror. And entirely alone.

Helen burst into the cramped cabin, they both stared at each other with vastly conflicting expressions on their faces.

Andy eventually broke the voiceless silence. "For God's sake, who am I?"

A week later Andy had checked into a clinic on the outskirts of Sydney. He spent six weeks in the hospice which dealt with all forms of neuroses.

Doctor Marcia Hendrix smilingly told the family that Andy should make a complete recovery. "By the way folks, how about a cup of camomile tea? I think you might need it". Dr Hendrix lost her giddy smile as she advised them that Andy would have to be on medication for some time, maybe for ever. "He has suffered a complete mental breakdown, frankly, my advice to all of you is, well, he should consider a change in lifestyle." The doctor regained her beatific smile as she advised the gathered throng. "Andy doesn't like people very much; I don't believe he has great faith in them." She poured the tea [with fresh lemon juice, obviously] for all the Piermont's. "It's something he will have to face from now on," she smilingly advised.

With the help of the good Dr Hendrix and a great number of unpronounceably named drugs, Andy made a commendable recovery whilst at the clinic, he also started to get back into shape. Dr Hendrix was proud of him and secretly felt that he may well be one of the patients that kicked the feared 'black dog' to the curb.

Sometime later, they were back in their comfy Sydney home, acting as though, virtually nothing had happened.

It was just two months later when Andy happily marched into the kitchen and announced, to Helen, that he was keen to relocate to Queensland and start a new life there. What he actually meant was, take over The Good Sportz business on the, Gold coast.

Everyone knew, Of course, that he would be taking over an already well-established going concern, with all the hard, creative work, done by previous managers.

Naturally, that never even crossed Andy's mind.

At least it would be a new start for the family!! Absolutely marvellous for everyone.

With the exception of young Stephen of course. He hated the idea and made it obvious that, A, he didn't want to go, he would miss his pals, and B, he would make his parents pay a dreadful price.

Andy had no idea why, but in fact, Helen was over the moon about the move, she had heard, on the grapevine, that QLD offered more opportunities for enthusiastic; youngish headmistresses, than any other state in Australia. So, off to sunny QLD. The state of warm weather, cheap mangoes, and a new start.

Chapter three.

For the first few years Helen easily found employment in the QLD education deptartment as a teacher, and that was fine, she still loved teaching children and was beginning to find the older students really stimulating, but her ambition had never wavered, and most months she wrote to the department applying for any headmistress position that was available.

So, the shade of that cool jacaranda tree helped to retain one of the exciting memories of her life.

Would she would accept the position?

You bet your sweet life she would.

That night she got all the family together to give them the news.

It was only later, as Helen thought about it, when she realised that Andrew, in retrospect, didn't really give a damn.   But he at least, tried to sound enthusiastic, unlike Young Stephen who hardly said a word, apart from a few noncomplimentary grunts, which was pretty much par for the course of late.

But, in his way, Stephen was relatively honest.

Regardless of family sarcasm, the next day Helen wrote to the school's board, and expressed her delight at being accepted for the appointment, and added that she was looking forward to meeting the committee at their convenience.

The situation was about as perfect as it could be. The school was less than 12 kilometres away, situated in a pleasant leafy part of the coast's hinterland. It was a multi lingual institution which catered for the growing ethnic population that was gracing QLD of late.

Wow, brilliant! She would be able to polish up her French and Italian language. Unfortunately, no Asian tongue.

Ah well, you can't have everything!

Helen was excited as she met with the Education committee and listened attentively to all the plans, they had for her. She was thrilled to learn that initially they expected her to attend a meeting in Kwinana, just south of Fremantle, in Western Australia,

The committee chairman, Dr Haywood, very kindly, but expressly advised Helen that they wanted her to present a paper to the committee instructors, as a representative of the QLD education academy. It would become part of their assessment of her suitability.

Her subject would be, 'How to Educate Young People, of Both Genders, to Understand the Developing State of Equality, Particularly with Respect to the Future Environment'.

Helen was thrilled. It was her theme in life. She knew exactly what she wanted to say. The delivery was to be 20 minutes long, with 5 minutes of questions afterwards. It was right up her alley.

In truth, she had been writing it all her life!

Nevertheless, it had to be right! Helen composed it, and then rewrote it, then she revised it, and then, after a great deal of thought, she completely rewrote it again, and again. Helen insisted that her husband acted as her audience.

She   delivered her lecture to Andrew… twice. To her son… once.   And, most importantly, to her dog Mr Biaggio, who was the only one who showed any real understanding, he developed a deep frown on his, blue heeler, forehead that made him look completely entranced.

Smart dog.   He was well fed that night!!

At last Helen felt that it was pretty close to OK.

Less than three weeks later Helen found herself at the Gold Coast airport, packed and ready to take on the world, or at least a critical cluster of pedagogues in WA.   The delightful Dr Haywood and his staff were there to bid them bon voyage amidst lots of laughter and handshakes.

Neither Andrew nor Stephen was at the airport.

This was her first visit to the enigmatic West Australian state.

As the plane flew over the coast, she could see the incredible blue Indian Ocean. Helen smilingly thought that it looked a lot like the blue waters of the Greek islands.

It didn't matter how you looked at it. It was….
Wow!

They landed at Perth airport to be met by the contingency from the W.A education department. Everyone seemed to know each other, Apart from Helen of course, each of them smiling and laughing. Eventually, Helen was delighted as they drew her into the gang, their welcoming friendliness helped to make her feel very quickly at home.

They were all staying at the Stagmart Hotel overlooking the ocean in Rockingham, about 30 kilometres south of Perth, and at least 7 degrees cooler, thank heavens!

The following morning, whilst they enjoyed a continental breakfast, they discovered that they were to be divided into groups of four.   From then on, they would be known as the wagtails.

Fair enough.

Helen told her, three fellow wagtails, that she would be delivering her paper next day. She tried very hard to make it sound flippant and an everyday part of her life.   The others smiled understandingly, Harry leant over and squeezed her hand.   They reminded her that each of them understood how much effort she had put into it her address. 'You'll be fine, just trust yourself.'

Good idea folks!

Next morning Helen donned a pair of grey gabardine slacks and a simple white shirt.   She gazed at her reflection in the mirror, and rather quizzically, decided that her image was vaguely reminiscent of the sensible shoes brigade. Helen immediately included a lovely brooch that Andrew had given her as a birthday present, and added a scarf effervescently coloured pink and yellow.

Yes, that'll do!

Later that morning when her name was called, she marched purposefully on to the stage, her ears ringing with the hearty cheers of the remaining wagtails. Don't think about it. Do it!

A very important 25 minutes in her life!!

Afterwards, as she waltzed off the stage, she knew that she held them in the palm of her hands, in retrospect she didn't really need the five minutes of post questioning.   She had hit the bullseye without even aiming.

The audience showed their appreciation by warmly applauding, but her fellow wagtails put their arms around her and kissed her.   Nothing needed to be said. Harry just gave the thumbs up sign and blew a kiss.

The four wagtails were teachers from all over Australia, Harry taught in Adelaide, both Sylvia and Donald were from WA and of course, Helen completed the quartet by happily hailing from QLD. They quickly became firm pals. Reliable to a fault.

Almost!

Harry suggested that they should celebrate that evening, by dining at the finest Korean restaurant in WA, which, by sheer luck, happened to be in Rockingham. He advised that they try the best 'chap chai, cellophane noodle stir-fry',
anywhere.   Including Korea!

Well, maybe that's a slight exaggeration, but absolutely delicious. They would serve Korean wine that was mind bogglingly good, so yes, let's do it.   We'll make it a celebration, a right old rave up!

Helen decided to get a bit dressed up for the evening, she donned her silk L.B.D. with her single strand of natural pearls.   Her dress was quite lovely and with just a hint of décolleté.

Helen was stunning.

They took a taxi into Rockingham town and, and headed straight to the famous restaurant. Frankly, they made a bit of a smash as they allowed themselves to be seated at the centre table in the dining room.   They began the meal with a glass of Korean wine that was very sweet, but ok, once you got used to it.   And boy, they got used to it, with a vengeance!

Ah well, a celebration was called for!

After the meal Harry suggested that they walk back to the hotel and have coffee in his room to discuss tomorrow's programme.

Well why not?

On the way to the hotel, Donald told a rather long joke which somehow used every really crude word you could think of.   It was absolutely filthy, they loved it, and all roared with laughter, like naughty schoolchildren.

Once they were back in the hotel, and a little more restrained, they headed for Harry's room.

Just before they arrived, Donald received a call on his mobile. He excused himself.   After a short while he returned and spoke rather secretly to Sylvia.   He confronted the other two and explained that they had an emergency and both them would have to leave pretty much immediately.   They were very sorry. 'I feel as if we're letting you both down', Donald appeared to be absolutely shattered.

For some reason or other, Sylvia less so.

As for the wagtails… And then there were two! By this time, they had arrived at Harry's room, he turned to Helen and just said, 'coffee'?

It turned out that Harry wasn't exactly employed as a headmaster, his position was to take the place of those teachers that were going on a sabbatical, or, indisposed for some reason or another. Harry found it perfect, he was unmarried and somewhat of an adventurer.   And, well it suited him.   He loved to travel, hence there was virtually no school in S.A that he didn't know. He grinned as he explained that he had a similar understanding with just about every vineyard and wine cellar. And there were lots of them in South Australia.

His room was a bit of a mess. Helen cheerfully recognised a bachelor pad when she saw one. Harry brought two cups of very strong, sweet Arabic style coffee for both of them, he didn't even ask Helen if that was her choice, it wouldn't have mattered anyway, that's all he had!   Harry obviously wanted to talk, he closed his eyes and told Helen about his life plans.   In fact, he didn't want to teach for very much longer. A few years ago, he found a perfect piece of land near Kersbrook. As far he was concerned it was the most ideal place to grow the best Grenache grapes in Australia, He smiled at Helen and asked her if she would like to try a glass of wine.   Helen nodded, of course she would.   Harry produced a bottle. 'It's called Ceschi   and quite delicious' he poured each of them a very large glass', He consulted the label. 'Actually, in Australia we call it chianti! I do hope you like it. Have you ever tried it before?''

Helen looked at him for a couple of minutes, just nodded and thoughtfully said, it was one of her favourites. As they both drank the delicious wine.

Chapter four.

Almost five years later, Helen had been appointed as headmistress to her chosen school, the very one at which she started her life's ambition.

A big tick for aspiration.

The home she lived in was lovely. She drove the car of her dreams. Andrew was relatively fit, and healthy. Young Stephen was continuously acting like a teenager, albeit a, surly sixteen-year-old know all.   So, everything was, pretty normal at home.

Her life should be very fulfilling!

But, 'It ain't necessarily so!'

One very important event, little Phoebe was nearly five years old, a delightful, happy child, who literally adored everyone in the family, particularly, her heroic, and, very gorgeous, but aloof, brother Stephen. He could do no wrong in her eyes. He was actually perfect.

But young Phoebe couldn't understand why Mummy and Daddy hardly ever spoke to each other, they weren't unpleasant, they simply ignored one another, and openly lived in separate parts of the house.

Very odd----- Why?

Phoebe had just started kindergarten. She felt very grown up. It was one of those schools where you didn't have to wear a uniform. Hooray!! She didn't actually know what uniforms were anyway.   But if her school didn't have them, then, they must be absolute rubbish.

Phoebe was potty over her school, all those new friends! It was marvellous. The preparatory school she attended was less than six hundred meters away from Stephen's rather imposing senior school.

But hers was far better because her favourite teacher, Miss Singh, was simply the best teacher in the world. And that's all there was to it.

Mummy insisted that she should hold Stephen's hand on the way, to and from, school, she thought it was ok, but Stephen was not so keen.   Ah well, maybe he would change one day.

The wondrous Miss Singh, was the lady who knew how to teach, absolutely everything, and make it fun, even sums. Miss Singh taught them the rules of the road, and she made everyone laugh when she pulled a funny face.

One morning, she took them to the edge of the pavement and, pretended that some traffic was coming. She explained what to do.

Actually, she was quite serious about this lesson.

First, you stand on the pavement and you don't move, next, you look to the left, then to the right, and then you look to the left again.   And, most importantly, if there is any traffic coming, you wait patiently till it has passed.   Then you do the exercise all over again.   Miss Singh insisted that we repeat everything she had taught us.

The beautiful Miss Singh didn't smile once. So, we knew it was extremely important... because she told us!

She was gorgeous and kind, and funny, and clever. Oh yes, and she always had a supply of jelly babies with her. So super!

It was just before the Christmas break, a warm day on the gold coast, Stephen and Phoebe were going to school for the last time before the Christmas holidays. Helen watched as the kids crossed the road. Stephen saw two of his mates and shouted to them, and then threw a ball to them and ran over.

Phoebe remembered her lessons and waited. Helen called out to her. 'Hold your brother's hand'.

No one saw the ute coming around the corner.

Phoebe, so confused, ran to her brother.

The utility driver was in no way at fault, trying frantically to brake as it crashed into little Phoebe. She was thrown into the air and landed on the hard pavement; her head took most of the impact.

The split-second silence was the longest in Christendom. Helen, Stephen and the distraught ute driver all got to Phoebe at the same time.

Stephen knelt beside his sister and whispered. 'Oh my god, she's dead', the driver shook his head and said, 'No she isn't, she's very badly hurt but she's still with us'. Helen shook with emotional horror; she immediately removed her coat and covered her baby with it.

One of the bystanders had phoned the emergency services. An ambulance was already on its way.

The poor ute driver collapsed and fell to the ground, the colour had drained from his face. Phoebe didn't move. Her little head was covered in blood but her eyes were flickering somewhat.

The ambulance officers, and the police arrived and immediately took charge over the accident. The ambo's stabilised the child and told the family to move back so that they could attach the wee lass to the lifesaving apparatus.

The ambo's told Helen that Phoebe was very badly hurt, but, with the immediate treatment she would get at the hospital, they felt that she stood a very good chance of survival. They quickly put Phoebe on to a stretcher and got her into the ambulance. Helen virtually begged that she and

Stephen be allowed to go to the hospital with Phoebe.

By now, the police had arrived and talked to the driver of the ute, the distraught fellow couldn't stop shaking. The chief ambo' agreed to let the ute driver accompany the ambulance to the hospital, with, of course, the immediate family.

Not one word was spoken on the way to the hospital. They accepted that they could do nothing, the ambulance operators were superbly efficient, and they were in constant contact with the hospital. As the ambulance pulled into the hospital grounds. Phoebe was immediately transferred to the emergency ward. Helen had phoned Andrew and broken the news to him. He instantly dropped everything and came to the hospital.

Phoebe was placed in an induced coma and she stayed that way for nearly a month. Slowly but surely her strong little body got better. The accident had caused her to fracture her skull and that was the most worrying aspect of her injuries, she had also cracked two ribs and broken one of her pelvic bones,   but it was the damage to her brain that was what concerned the medics.

The family insisted that one of them had to be by her side all the time, they didn't want her to wake up and be frightened to be alone.

It was nearly a month later and Stephen was sitting next to Phoebe, her eyes flickered and she looked around and said, 'Where's my mummy'? Stephen smiled at her and said, 'she'll be here very soon.' Phoebe nodded and said, 'Well, I'm hungry.'

In fact, both Andrew and Helen were in the doctor's office. He smilingly explained, 'Actually we're very pleased with young Phoebe's progress, the concussion isn't as bad as we thought, the problem she faces is being in a brace for a while until her bones strengthen   and that could take three months'. He rather seriously explained, 'We have removed the bandages on her head and, frankly, well, she looks like she has been in a fight with superman and lost, but that will clear up soon. Now I think we should go to the ward and cheer her up a bit. Oh and by the way she told me this morning that she wants to be a doctor, when she grows up, either that or a bus driver'.

Less than three weeks, after her first awakening she was looking much more like the Phoebe they knew and loved.

She had received lots of cards from her friends at school and the rest of the family in Sydney. Oh yes, and very oddly, one from someone in South Australia… So, things were pretty good really.

One Saturday afternoon mummy and daddy were at the end of the bed when Stephen came in and announced that he had a really whopping big surprise. It was an enormous bunch of flowers which camouflaged the carrier, who was of course, Miss Singh, and Phoebe's very best two friends from school, Monica and Hilary, they had got dressed up in Zombie costumes, including the ugliest masks you've ever seen. They both walked in a daft way and made funny noises as they waddled all around the hospital ward. Phoebe thought they were marvellous and she screeched with laughter.

She held her mummy's hand and whispered that she was feeling a whole lot better.   Then told her, in strictest confidence that she wanted to be a teacher when she's a bit older. 'Just like you'. Helen put on her teachers face and said. 'I thought you wanted to be a bus driver.' Phoebe shook her head and explained, very seriously, 'Oh mummy, that was yesterday.'

Life was about as good as it could be.

About the author

Jeremy John Lowley---Jerry to his friends,
English by birth and Australian by attitude.

 Rather than bore you to tears, my life really
hasn't been that flabbergastingly interesting,
maybe I should list the things that delight me:

* Starting with my family, a daughter and a
granddaughter, both absolutely beautiful.

* Live theatre, both drama and of course
comedy.

* Cricket, all forms, although I'm not quite sure
about twenty/twenty but I suppose that it's the
future of the game---so!!

* Living in QLD, where else would you choose?

* Good Italian red wine---Chianti by choice, but
really an Aussie Cab/Sav takes a bit of beating.
* I enjoy a massive love of good sportsmanship;
my simple philosophy is that any sport played
without honour literally isn't worth the effort.
Sorry; but that's the way I feel.

* People of course--- that is; until we come up with something better; well we're stuck with us!!

* Oh yes, creative art. Just imagine a world without it!

* Music. Ditto creative art.

* The Broncos, well someone's got to care.

Other books by the author:

Plays:
49 Not Out
The Lady in Suite 57
Two for the Price of One